Great
Expectations

Written by Hilary McKay

Illustrated by Stefano Tambellini

Collins

I didn't have great expectations.

I didn't have any expectations.

I had a great many trembly fears.

I spent a lot of time in
the graveyard. It's the first place
I remember. Not the forge,
with the red fire and the low
roof and the wild bare
marsh all around.
Not the wet, rutty road that
led to the village and then
to the town and then on to
far-off wonders: London,
perhaps, or the end of
the world.

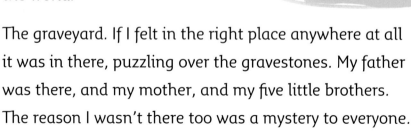

The graveyard. If I felt in the right place anywhere at all
it was in there, puzzling over the gravestones. My father
was there, and my mother, and my five little brothers.
The reason I wasn't there too was a mystery to everyone.

I lived at the forge with Joe and Mrs Joe. My trembly fears were the result of living with Mrs Joe.

The small warm feeling I had of not being quite alone in the world came from living with Joe.

"Ever the best of friends, eh Pip?" said Joe.

Pip – that was me.

Chapter 2

Joe was the blacksmith who worked the forge. He was very big and I was very small, but we understood each other. We also shared a problem. Our problem was Mrs Joe, and Mrs Joe's temper, which was sometimes very fiery. Neither Joe nor I could do much about it, but we put up with it together. And Mrs Joe put up with us – just.

I was a great trouble to Mrs Joe. If I was in the house, I was under her feet. If I was out of the house, she couldn't rest for worrying what mischief I might find. Because of this, Mrs Joe became very good at finding jobs to keep me out of trouble. She found me one on Christmas Eve. She sent me to the graveyard to tidy round the graves.

It was very quiet in the graveyard.

Some of the gravestones were so huge they loomed high over my head. Others had slipped in the marshy ground and hung at impossible angles, waiting to fall. There were gravestones so old that time had worn them half away, and gravestones so new they looked raw.

My family's gravestones still looked raw.

I couldn't cry at the forge. It worried Joe and it angered Mrs Joe. But I could cry as much as I liked in the graveyard. And since it was Christmas Eve and grey and damp, and the wind was cold and I was all alone, that's what I did.

I sniffed and then rubbed my eyes with my muddy hands. My tears came faster and faster. It seemed to me that my tears were the only warm thing in the whole cold landscape, and that thought made me more sorry for myself than ever.

And so I settled down to a good, noisy, wail.

A thin mist crept in from
the marsh to listen.

"HOLD YOUR NOISE!"

I leapt in terror.

The bellow had come from
the shadows by the wall.
The shadows moved and
became a terrible figure.
A man. Perhaps.

He looked like a man freshly
dragged out from the soaking
earth. Drenched. Ragged.
Cold as clay. His hands gripped
my arms and his hoarse voice said
he might cut my throat. I believed every word.

But he didn't cut my throat. He tipped me upside down
to empty my pockets. I kept a piece of bread with me
when I could, to throw to a savage, starving dog that
guarded a nearby farm. The terrible man ate that dry
crust as if he might die if he didn't. And he mentioned
that he might also eat me.

I believed that too. I had never met a man who so plainly spoke the truth.

He was a prisoner, escaped.

I knew that when I saw his leg with the iron ring around it. A chain was fixed to the ring, and a great iron ball, bigger than my head, bigger than his head, dragged from the chain.

The man told me what he wanted: food and a file.

"You know what a file is?" he asked me.

I knew what a file was because Joe had them at the forge. It was a tool that would saw through iron. If the man sawed with a file for long enough, he could cut through the ring on his leg.

Food and a file – I was to bring them in the morning and tell no one.

Or he'd have my heart and liver.

That's what he said, and then he let me go.

9

I didn't want to steal from Joe. I liked him too much.
I didn't want to steal from fiery-tempered Mrs Joe either,
but that night I did both. Not just because I was afraid
not to.

That was not the whole reason. Almost, but not quite.

I'd been cold, but he'd been colder. I'd been hungry, but he was ravenous. I'd thought I was alone, but he was the loneliest person I'd ever met. And he was frightened. I thought he was as frightened as me.

I stole the file and I stole bread and cheese. And I stole, since Mrs Joe would go wild anyway, the big, brown, once-a-year-at-Christmas prize pork pie.

I thought he would enjoy it if he was still there in the morning.

He was still there. Colder, shaking with cold.
Hungrier, shaking with that too. But he enjoyed his pie.
I asked him, and he told me. "Thankee, my boy,"
he said.

And he asked my name.

And I told him, Pip.

Then I left, because I was
afraid to spend any more
time away.

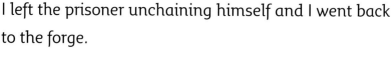

"Give us the file, boy."

That was the last thing
he said to me.

He didn't say goodbye.
He didn't watch me go.
He was filing away at his iron ring.

He was like the savage dog at the farm. I was sorry
for him, and I was terrified of him. I would never have
dared unchain him.

I left the prisoner unchaining himself and I went back
to the forge.

Later that day, I learnt his name: Magwitch.
Soldiers came hunting for Magwitch all over the marsh.
Mrs Joe instantly blamed him for the loss of
the pork pie. Magwitch must have stolen it.

"Poor fellow," said kind Joe.

I didn't say anything.

Chapter 3

For a long time, my nights were haunted.

My days, however, were still a problem to poor Mrs Joe.
When I was big enough I would work with Joe at
the forge, and in those days, I thought that was
the best thing that could happen to a boy. But for now,
while I was still not much higher than Joe's elbow,
I was not much help as a blacksmith. However,
Mrs Joe was determined to find a use for me. She let it
be known in the village that if any person needed a boy
for odd jobs, she had one ready and waiting.

I had many odd jobs.
I minded babies. I was
a real live scarecrow
for the farmer with
the savage dog. I picked
up stones from the fields
and helped an ancient

neighbour with her annual washing of her sheets.

I became quite famous for the oddness of my jobs,
and in this way, I was given the oddest of all.

Miss Havisham.

In our nearest town, the only town I had ever seen, lived a strange woman. Everyone knew of her, but hardly anyone ever saw her. She was very rich and very scary and she lived in a great dark shabby house with her adopted daughter, Estella. And Estella needed company. A boy to play with. Me.

Joe didn't like the idea, but Mrs Joe did. She thought if Miss Havisham liked me, it might be a wonderful thing. Perhaps one day a part of her money might come to me. Perhaps I might not always be a poor boy. Perhaps Joe might not always be a poor blacksmith. Perhaps Mrs Joe might not always be a poor blacksmith's wife.

Mrs Joe began to have expectations.

17

And so I was sent to Miss Havisham's house, every day, to play. Miss Havisham, whose yellow skin had not seen daylight for years. Whose face was a skull. Whose eyes were dark fire. Who wore the remains of the wedding dress she had put on twenty years before and never taken off. Whose wedding feast sat on the table still, green with rot, grey with cobwebs. The wedding that had never happened.

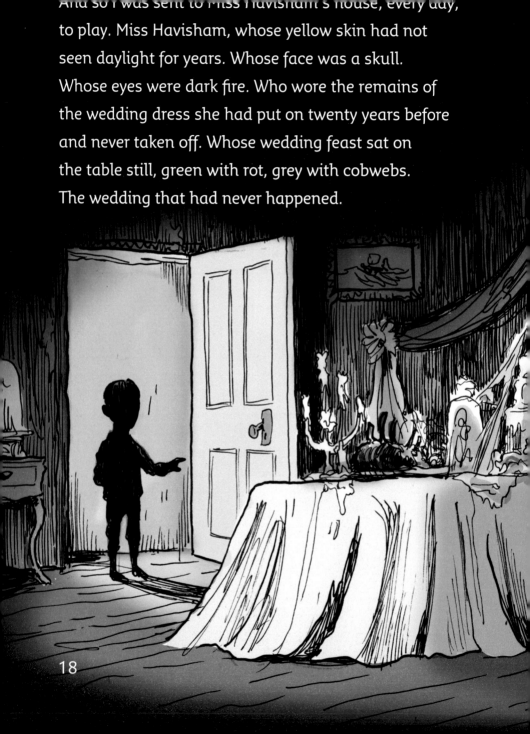

Miss Havisham's heart, she told me fiercely,
was broken.

Miss Havisham called me "boy".

So did Estella.

Estella was bigger than me in those days, and she was
beautiful. Starry. She gleamed. She was like a cool clear
light in that dark house.

Estella laughed at me.

I became ashamed of my thick boots, and my red chapped hands. I became ashamed of my home and the way we lived there. Even the ways we talked and walked and ate. I began to notice how Joe smelt of the smoke and iron of the forge.

I even became ashamed of Joe.

Chapter 4

Very soon, Miss Havisham and Estella were the only people who mattered much to me.

It hadn't taken me long to fall in love with Estella.

Miss Havisham watched.

I thought she was pleased.

I wanted to please her very much indeed.

Usually Estella was rude to me. Often she laughed at me. But once, after a particularly hard day, she surprised me completely.

She turned her cheek to me and told me I could kiss her.

So I did.

One day, I thought, when I was grown, I would rescue Estella from her strange life. The great, awful house would be made all fresh and new. Miss Havisham would throw away her wedding feast and buy a new dress. Estella and I would live happily ever after.

How would I do this?

I didn't quite know.

Except that Estella had said I could kiss her.

And sometimes Miss Havisham smiled as she watched us together.

I began to have expectations of my own. Not great ones – still quite small ones.

23

Time went by. Nothing changed at the forge.
Nothing changed at Miss Havisham's house. But I,
to everyone's surprise, began to change and change.
I started to take on rich folk's ways. The way they talked.
The way they opened a door, or held a knife.
I started to see that it would be a good thing to learn
to read and write. I worked at that, at night by the fire.
Joe was soon astonished at the amount I knew. It was
very little, but it was very much more than him.

Also I grew, past Joe's elbow and up to his shoulder. Suddenly, I was big enough to work at the forge.

When I was little, it had seemed the best thing that could happen to me.

Now it seemed the worst.

I thought Miss Havisham might save me, but she didn't. I was old enough to go back to the forge, and big enough to go back to the forge, and that had always been the future planned for me, so back to the forge I went.

Only Joe was happy. Joe's round face shone like the sun.
He'd looked forward to teaching me for years and years.

"Ever the best of friends, eh Pip!" said Joe.

I suppose I nodded, but I'd grown out of the old life.
I didn't want to smell of smoke and iron like Joe.

It was strange being back at the forge again.
Miss Havisham and Estella had filled my thoughts.

Estella. I thought of her so often, but I never had a sign
to show that she remembered me.

I trudged through a year, and then another, and then everything changed! Wonderful news! A lawyer came all the way from London with a message. I was to be educated as a gentleman. There was money to spend. There was a place for me in London, ready and waiting.

All I had to do was ask no questions, because
the person who had arranged all this for me was
a private sort of person.

I didn't ask questions, but I went
to thank Miss Havisham.
I knelt and thanked her,
and she smiled.

Chapter 5

I left the forge and I went to London. There are a lot of mistakes a boy can make in London when he has too much money in his pocket. I don't think I left many out. I think I pretty nearly made them all.

Once Joe came to see me, all shining in his best clothes with hardly a smell of smoke or iron about him. Just a whiff.

Anyway, he saw how I'd grown, and he noticed I smelt that whiff of the forge, and he didn't stay too long to embarrass me.

Estella was sometimes in London, visiting friends and, I guessed, escaping the lonely life she lived with Miss Havisham. I saw her now and then (never often enough) and she was almost the same as ever. Cool and starry, but now also a little sad. I found that I wasn't the only person who longed to rescue her from her life at home. London, it seemed, was full of bright young fellows with exactly that idea.

"Because I'm rich," said Estella, coolly.

I was not too worried because I thought I was the chosen one. I had thought of rescuing Estella first, and I was the one who was going to live happily ever after with her. Why else was I in London, learning to be a gentleman? Why else had Miss Havisham smiled when I knelt and thanked her?

Oh, I thought a lot of myself! I really did have great expectations.

Time rushed away in London. Time and money!

The money that rushed through my pockets in a week
would have lasted Joe for a year. I bought myself
the best of the best, because that was what I thought
I deserved.

Then I got what I deserved.

I had a visitor.

I found out where the money had come from.

Not Miss Havisham. Poor Miss Havisham, mad since
her empty wedding day, playing with people, and
watching people play. She had smiled when I knelt
and thanked her because she was amused.
The common boy from the forge, believing he was
the one for Estella! That was why she smiled.

So who was I to Estella now?

No one.

No more than all the other bright young men who
followed her around.

"Because I'm rich," said Estella, a little sadly.

Chapter 6

The night I got what I deserved, the last night of my great expectations, Magwitch arrived at my door.

Magwitch was my visitor.

36

Not long after his visit to our village, Magwitch had been recaptured. His punishment for his escape had been to be sent to Australia. It was a terrible punishment in those days, to be sent to the other side of the world. The ships were so bad that many prisoners died on the journey. More died from the life they had to live there afterwards. But a few found work and somehow survived.

Magwitch was one of them.

Magwitch, who had eaten our Christmas pork pie, and had been so grateful for it, and for my few words of kindness that long ago Christmas morning – he had never forgotten me. He worked and worked, and saved and saved. He had made quite a lot of money, and he had saved it all for me.

Magwitch had sent the money to turn me into
a gentleman, and now he had travelled the long
journey back again to admire the results.

Magwitch looked at me with pride and love when he told me all this.

I did not look at him with love. I could have howled.

But it was no use howling, because Magwitch was ill and he had no one to help him except me, whether I liked it or not.

I didn't like it, but I did it.

Looking after Magwitch started me at last on
the long road to growing up. The story of his brave,
ruined life, and all the terrible happenings that
had led him to the graveyard where he and
I first met, was the saddest I ever heard.
I looked after him until he died, and
by that time I cared just as much
for him as he did for me.

When Magwitch died there was no more money, and so I went back to the forge.

And after all the time I had been in London, and the miserable way I had treated Joe, this is what he said when I turned up penniless on his doorstep.

"Ever the best of friends, eh Pip?"

And hugged me.

Money does not make a gentleman. Courage and kindness do that. Courage like Magwitch's, kindness like Joe's.

Miss Havisham died, and her house burnt down. I was the common boy at the forge again, and Estella seemed as far away as a star.

I thought she must have forgotten me.

I could not forget her, and one day I went to look at the place where we first met. Miss Havisham's house. The garden was a wilderness around the blackened ruins.

And there she was, walking in the garden. Estella.

The same starry Estella, but grown up now, like me.

She hadn't forgotten me.

I think right from the beginning we had been meant for each other, I for Estella, and Estella for me. That was how it seemed to us both, when we met in the garden that day.

So we came to a happy ever after, after all.

Pip becomes a gentleman

The small warm feeling I had of not being quite alone in the world came from living with Joe.

Money does not make a gentleman. Courage and kindness do that.

Looking after Magwitch started me at last on the long road to growing up.

... the last night of my great expectations, Magwitch arrived at my door.

I was sorry for him, and I was terrified of him.

It hadn't taken me long to fall in love with Estella.

A lawyer came all the way from London with a message. I was to be educated as a gentleman.

There are a lot of mistakes a boy can make in London when he has too much money in his pocket.

Ideas for reading

Written by Linda Pagett B.Ed (hons), M.Ed
Lecturer and Educational Consultant

Learning objectives: interrogate texts to deepen and clarify understanding and response; deduce characters' reasons for behaviour from their actions; explain how writers use figurative and expressive language to create images and atmosphere; comment constructively on performance

Curriculum links: History; Citizenship

Interest words: expectations, trembly, forge, file, ravenous, adopted, chapped, trudged, gentleman, penniless, wail

Resources: internet, paints, collage materials

Getting started

This book can be read over two or more reading sessions.

- Explain that this is a retelling of a book by Charles Dickens, a famous author. Investigate whether or not the children have any previous experience of this story and what they know of it.

- Invite a discussion of the title. Demonstrate using the word *expectations*, e.g. *I have great expectations that you will enjoy this story.*

- Invite one of the children to read the blurb and make predictions about the text, e.g. it is set a long time ago.

Reading and responding

- Demonstrate reading the first chapter aloud. Do this with expression and a critical approach, e.g. *I like the way that the beginning draws the reader in.*

- Direct the children to read Chapter 2 silently and then ask them to explain what more they have learnt of the characters.

- Invite children to choose a character and draw its face in the middle of a piece of paper. Then support them to write labels around the image as they read through the book, to describe the character's behaviour and characteristics.